This SKIN of Mine

Written by: Jenifer N. James,
LPC, CCTP, CAADC

Copyright © 2021 Jenifer N. James.

All rights reserved. No part of this publication may be reproduced, distributed, or transmitted in any form or by any means, including photocopying, recording, or other electronic or mechanical methods, without the prior written permission of the publisher, except in the case of brief quotations embodied in a book review.

ISBN: 978-1-7368307-2-7 (Paperback) 1st Ed.

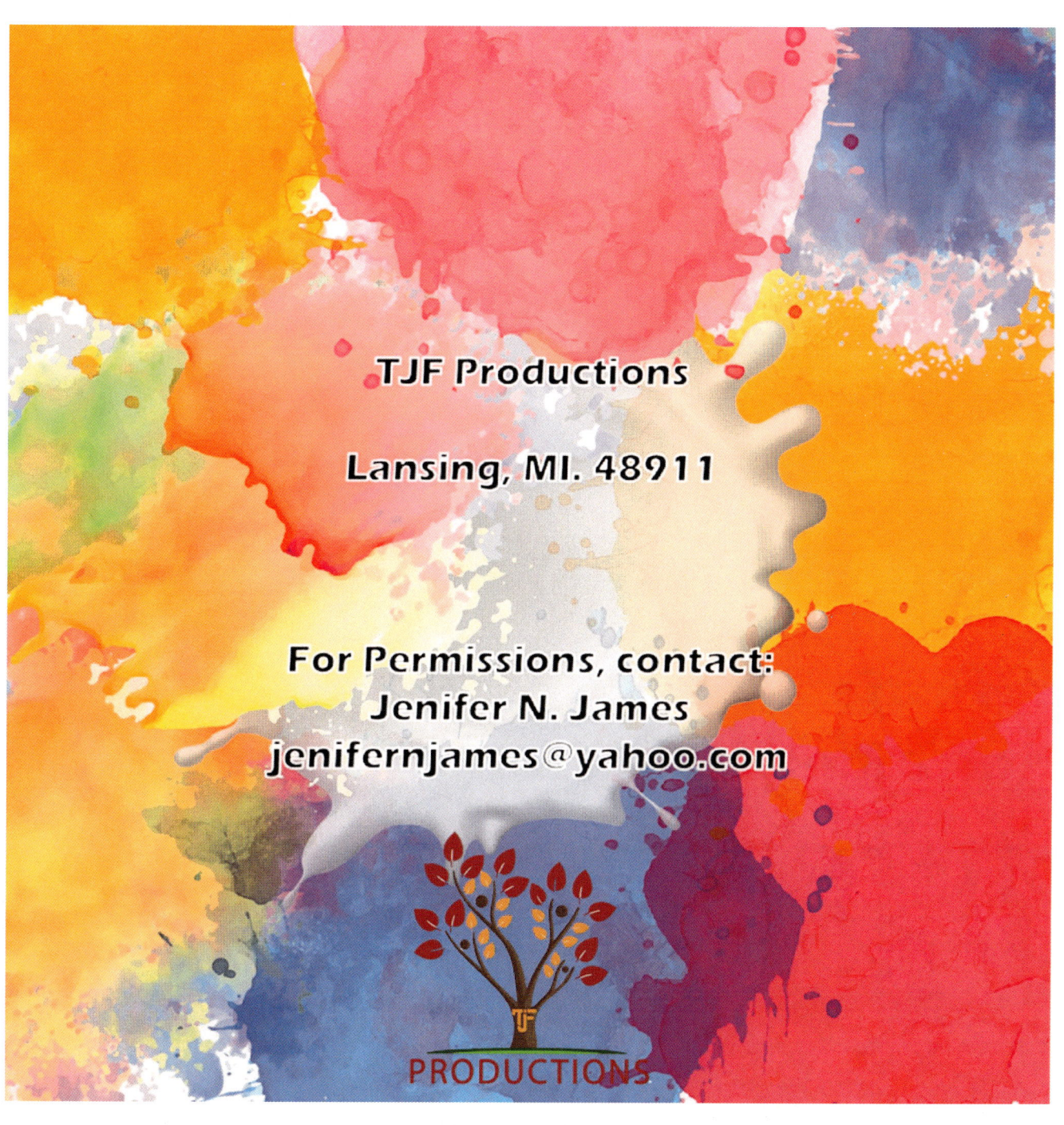

Dedication

This Skin of Mine is dedicated to every individual who has ever experienced discrimination because of the color of your skin or has struggled with identity associated with acceptance. You are beautiful, valuable, and worthy! Colorism or any "ism" is a tactic to distract you from accepting and loving your true self. Don't let them win! Who you are is invaluable and necessary for change. You were uniquely made !!!!

Jenifer N James, LPC, CCTP, CAADC
TJF Productions

I'm human, no doubt,

but my color has meaning.

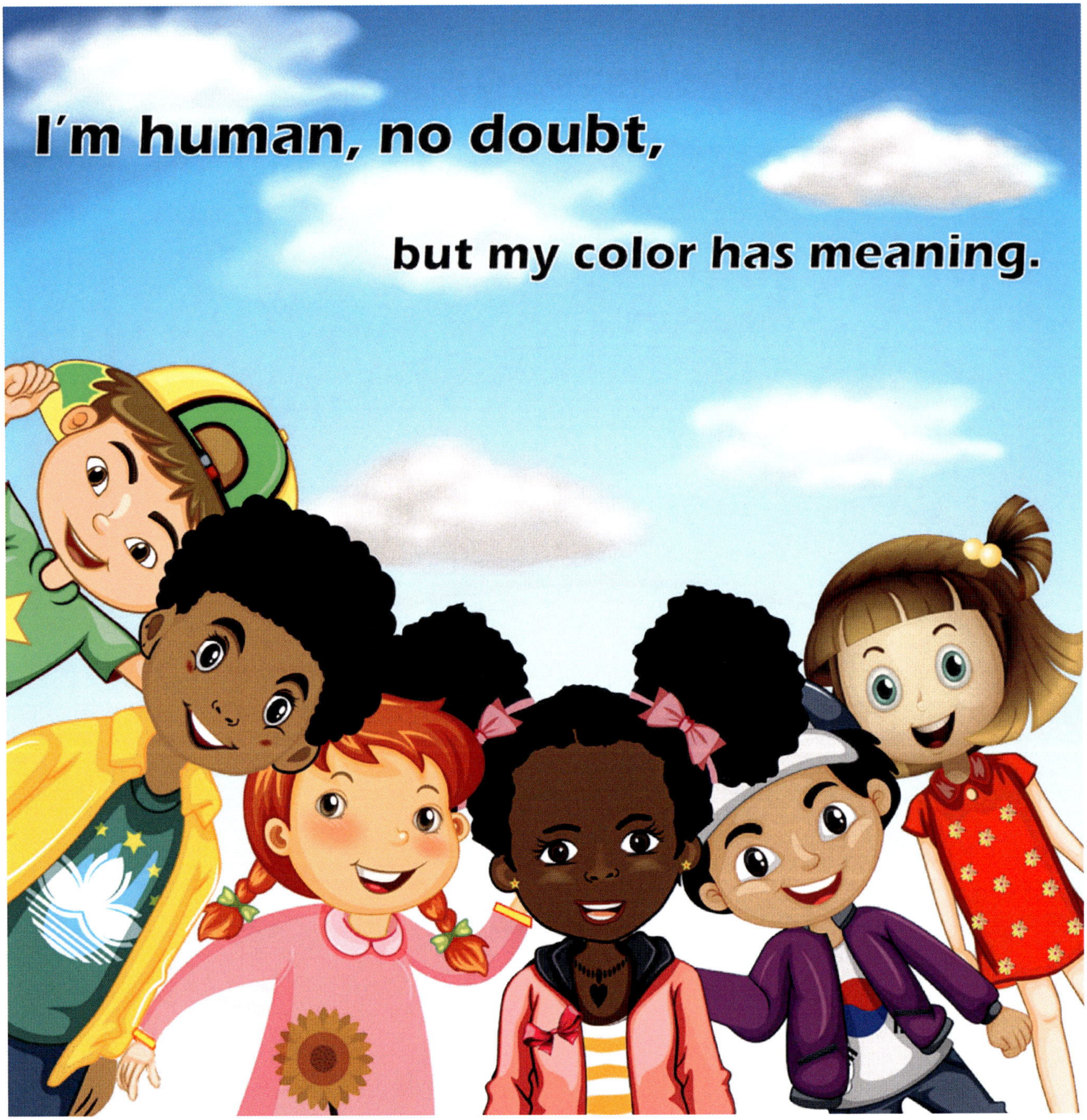

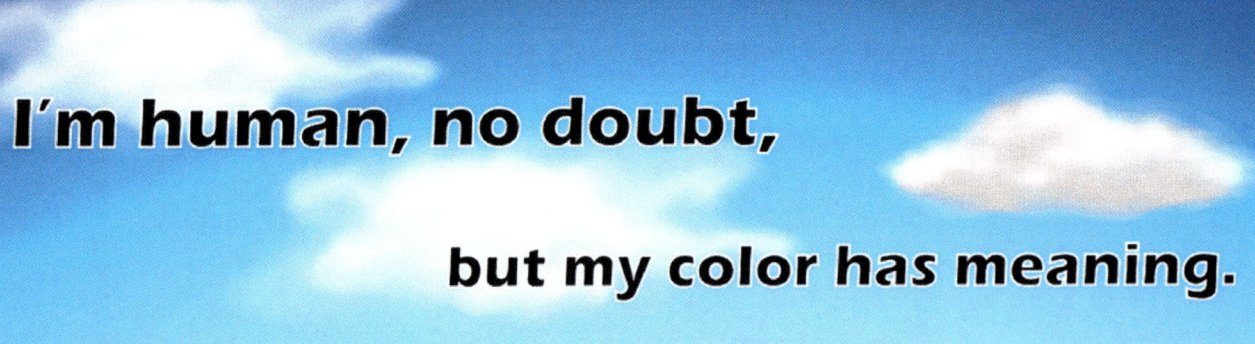

Made in the USA
Columbia, SC
05 May 2021